Three Ogre Hairs

Iranian Folk Tale

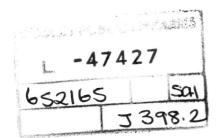

Three Ogre Hairs

Text/illustrations by Nayyereh Taghavi
Retold by Yuko Saito
English Text by Sean Nelson

Shinseken

"O King, somewhere in the kingdom a child has been born. This child has a mole on each shoulder. Someday he will become king, and you will be deposed." So said the astrologer.

The king was shocked to hear this and quickly sent word throughout the kingdom: "There will be a reward for the person who brings forth a baby with a mole on both shoulders."

Presently a wretched-looking man appeared carrying a baby.

"O King, as you can see, my son has a mole on both shoulders."

Smiling, the king gave a reward to the man and said, "What a fine boy! I'll take him into the castle and give him a fine upbringing."

The man had no choice but to obey his king's order. He returned, leaving his baby behind.

That evening the king secretly put the baby into a box and set it out into the river, then returned to the castle, relieved. But the box didn't sink! It bobbed along, carried downstream by the current, and eventually became caught in some reeds by the shore.

The next morning, an old miller discovered the box. "Oh my! God must have sent my poor wife and me the son we have always wanted."

The miller and his wife named the child "Behzad" and raised him in their watermill as if he were their own.

With the passage of time Behzad became a fine young man.

One day while hunting, the king and his servants chanced to pass by the watermill.

"I'm thirsty. Let's rest here a little," said the king, and he went into the watermill.

Behzad served his royal guest attentively and without hesitation. The king took a liking to him and asked him many questions. Then suddenly, the king recognized who he was talking to.

(Ah! This is the child I put into the river!)

Acting as if all was well, the king wrote onto a piece of paper:

"The person who brings this note to you is to be killed immediately."

Then he sealed the note and handed it to Behzad, saying:

"Deliver this to the queen for me."

Suspecting nothing, Behzad quickly mounted his horse and departed for the castle. Before long the sun set and a terrible rain started. In the darkness, drenched Behzad came across a house and knocked on the door.

"Good evening. I'm sorry to intrude, but do you think I could spend the evening here?"

An old woman came to the door. "You can stay, but thieves live here and I don't know what they'll do to you when they return."

Behzad chuckled and replied, "That's fine. I'm not afraid of thieves. Besides, I have nothing worth stealing."

The old woman showed Behzad in and set up a bed for him beside the fireplace. Behzad lay down and was quickly asleep.

The thieves returned in the middle of the night. "Hey, woman, who's this sleeping here?"

"It's a young traveler taking refuge from the rain."

The thieves went through Behzad's things and discovered the king's note. "What's this? The person who delivers this note is to be killed? How terrible! This poor fellow has no idea what's going to happen to him. Well, let's make a few changes..."

The thieves threw the note away and wrote a new one, imitating the king's writing exactly "The princess is to immediately marry the person who brings you this note so that he may become my son."

The next morning Behzad left the thieves' house and arrived at the castle. When he gave the note to the queen, she was surprised, but she had no choice but to obey the king's order. She arranged for the wedding and the princess was married to Behzad without delay.

The king soon returned and was shocked to find that Behzad was not only alive, but also married to his daughter. It seemed as if the astrologer's prediction was coming true and Behzad would soon replace the king.

So the king said: "Behzad, to become the husband of the princess there is a task you must complete. You must go and bring back three hairs from the head of an ogre. The marriage is not binding unless you can do this." Behzad was surprised. "But your Majesty, where can I find an ogre?" "I do not know," replied the king, "that is also part of your task."

Having no choice, Behzad set out to find an ogre. After he had walked for some time he saw a village with golden-colored walls. Behzad approached the guard who was watching over the entrance. "Good day. Do you by any chance know where I might find an ogre?" "Ogre?" puzzled the guard. "I'm afraid not. But I'm sure my brother would – he's very knowledgeable. You'll find him guarding the next village. By the way, if you do find an ogre, could you ask him something? Our village has an amazing tree that bore golden apples, but they no longer grow and nobody knows why. Surely an ogre would know."

Behzad continued to the next village, which had walls the color of sherbet. At the entrance was a guard who looked just like the other one. "Good day," said Behzad. "Do you by any chance know where I might find an ogre?" To which the guard replied, "I'm afraid not. But if you follow this path to its end, you'll find a lake. I'm sure the lake's ferryman will be able to answer your question – he's very knowledgeable. By the way, if you do find an ogre could you ask him something? Our village had a wonderful sherbet spring, but it's dried up and nobody knows why. Surely an ogre would know."

Behzad walked some more and came to a lake. Sure enough, a ferryman was standing in a boat by the shore. Behzad approached him. "Good day. Do you by any chance know where I might find an ogre?" "Ogre," pondered the ferryman, "ogre, you say? No doubt there's one living in the mountain cave on the other side of the lake."

Behzad boarded the boat and the ferryman took him to the other side. As they approached the far shore, he asked Behzad, "By the way, if you find an ogre please ask him how I can quit being a ferryman. I'm so tired of ferrying people back and forth, back and forth. Surely an ogre would know how I could quit."

Behzad climbed the mountain and found the cave. He knocked on the door and an old ogre woman appeared. "Oh my, what's this?" she said. "What's a human doing here? If my son comes home he'll eat you up just like that!"

Behzad told her his tale and she exclaimed, "My my, what a story! Well then, let me see what I can do for you." She used some magic to turn Behzad into a tiny ant, then she hid him in a pleat of her dress.

Before long her son returned. "Oh, what a delicious smell! A human-like smell. Was a human here today, mother?"

"What are you talking about," she said. "It's just this delicious meal I've prepared for you. Hurry up and eat, you must be hungry!"

Her son bolted down the entire meal. With a full stomach he laid him down to sleep using his mother's knee for a pillow.

Poink! The mother plucked a hair from her son's head. *Flick!* Her son's eyes shot open. "Mother, I dreamt that a bee stung me!" "Really?" said his mother. "Why I too had a strange dream. I dreamt of a village with a tree that bore golden apples, but the apples stopped growing and nobody knew why." "Oh, that tree?" said her son, half asleep. "Of course the apples are gone. A big mouse is harming the tree by gnawing at its roots." And with that he drifted back to sleep again.

Poink! The mother plucked a second hair from her son's head. *Flick!* Her son's eyes shot open. "Ow! Mother, I dreamt that I was stung again!" "Really?" said his mother. "I had another strange dream too. I dreamt of a village with a sherbet spring. But the spring dried up and nobody knew why." "Oh, that spring?" muttered her son groggily. "Of course it dried up. A toad lives at the base of the spring and he's plugged it up." Then her son put his head down once more and began to snore.

Poink! The mother plucked a third hair from her son's head. *Flick!* Her son's eyes shot open and he jumped right up. "Ouch, that was a dreadful sting! Mother, why do I keep having such a strange dream?" "Good heavens, really?" said his mother. "I had still another strange dream too. There was a ferryman going back and forth, back and forth, ferrying people across a lake. He wanted to quit, but didn't know how." "Oh, that ferryman?" mumbled the ogre, drifting back to sleep again. "It's really very simple. The next time someone gets into the boat, he should just hand the oars to that person and run away."

When her son went back to sleep, the mother turned Behzad back into a human and gave him her son's three hairs. Behzad thanked her and started back. When he arrived at the lakeshore, the ferryman asked, "How did it go? Did the ogre answer my question?" "Yes he did," said Behzad, "but please take me back to the other shore before I tell you what he said."

When the boat arrived at the other shore, Behzad leapt out and started to run. As he fled, Behzad called over his shoulder, "The next time someone gets into the boat, hand over the oars and run!"

When Behzad arrived at the village with the sherbet spring the guard asked him, "How did it go? Did the ogre answer my question?" "Yes he did. A toad at the base of the spring is plugging it up. If you kill it then the spring will start to flow again." The guard was very pleased and gave Behzad two donkeys and two bags of silver.

Behzad continued his journey and soon arrived at the village with the golden apple tree. "How did it go?" asked the guard. "Did the ogre answer my question?" "Yes he did. A mouse underneath the tree is gnawing at the roots. If you kill it then the apples will start to grow again." The guard was very happy and gave Behzad a sack of golden apples from the storehouse. And so by the time Behzad returned to the castle, he not only had the three ogre hairs, but also two donkeys, two bags of silver, and a bag of golden apples.

The king was very surprised. He thought: (This ogre can't be all that bad. Look what he gave that simple fellow. If I, the king, was to go, imagine the treasures he would give me!)

The king asked Behzad where the ogre lived and left immediately. Traveling quickly, he arrived at the lake and boarded the ferry boat.

The chance had come! The ferryman handed the oars to the king, who took them without thinking. Then the ferryman leapt to the shore and ran away.

Thus the king became the new ferryman. Since he didn't know how to quit, he spent the rest of his life ferrying people back and forth, back and forth across the lake.

And because the king never returned, Behzad succeeded him and from then on lived happily with his bride in the castle, just as the astrologer predicted.

Three Ogre Hairs

This story from Iran (formerly Persia) is very similar to a Slovakian folk tale, and might have made it's way from there to Germany to be retold by the brothers Grimm. The ferryman of the story could have plied his boat across the Black Sea. People in each of neighboring countries may well have believed that an ogre lived in the country on the opposite side.

Nayyereh Taghavi

Born in 1950. Bachelor of Fine Arts, Tehran University. Freelance illustrator and graphic designer. Named in the IBBY Honour List in 1988. Prize-winner in the first Tehran International Biennale of Illustrations 1991.

Yuko Saito

Born in 1949 in Shimane, Japan. After graduating from College she traveled for more than 10 years to a number of countries throughout the world. Her published works include *The Spirit of the Tree* and *Journey from Beyond.*

Three Ogre Hairs

2002年12月31日発行

再話・絵　　　Nayyereh Taghavi（ナイエレ・タガビ）

文　　　　　　Yuko Saito（さいとう ゆうこ）

訳　　　　　　Sean Nelson（ショーン・ネルソン）

デザイン　　　長谷川 公美／有薗 栄子

発行人　　　　M. クレスポ　　　　　　　印刷・製本　　（株）太平印刷社

発行所　　　　新世研　　　　　　　　　　定価　　　　　本体 2761円＋税

〒177-0041　東京都練馬区石神井町6-27-29　ISBN　　　　4-88012-895-3

TEL 03 (3995) 8871/ FAX 03 (5393) 0456　Printed in Japan

乱丁・落丁本は、お取り替えいたします。